The Magic
Motor Car

illustrated by
Chris Rothero

AWARD PUBLICATIONS LIMITED

Cherry Village was a very happy little place until Mister Bong came to live there. It was beautiful in the springtime when all the cherry trees were out, and it was fun to be there in the summer when the cherries were ripe. Then everyone had cherry-tart and cream.

But when Mister Bong came, he made himself a great nuisance. He talked so much. He borrowed such a lot of things from the village folk. He said such horrid things about them. In fact, he was very tiresome indeed.

'Here comes Mister Bong!' Gobo would say to Littlefeet. 'Quick! Let's run away before he sees us! He is sure to want to borrow something!'

And off they would go – but Mister Bong would be sure to grumble about something or other.

He loved to see anything new that the folk of Cherry Village bought. When Gogo brought home a new wireless set, Bong knocked at his door, walked in, and spent the whole evening twiddling the knobs of the set – though poor Gobo was longing to try it himself.

When Tiptoe bought a new bicycle, Mister Bong borrowed it, and rode it to Heyho Town to see his aunt – and when he brought it back the bell was broken.

'You ought to pay for a new bell,' said Tiptoe crossly. But Mister Bong just laughed, went home and banged his door. And Tiptoe had to pay for a new bell herself.

But when Mister Bong borrowed Dame Jelly's garden-roller without asking, and lost it in the village pond, everybody said something must be done about him.

'But how did he lose the roller in the pond?' asked Gobo in surprise. He had been away for the day and hadn't heard what had happened.

'Well, you see, he went to borrow the roller one night, when Dame Jelly was asleep,' said Tiptoe. 'And, as you know, her house is at the top of the hill. Well, just as he was setting off down the hill, Bong sneezed, and it was such a big sneeze that he let go of the roller. It rolled by itself at a great speed down the hill, and went splash right into the pond.'

'And as the pond is big and deep, we can't see it anywhere, so it's quite lost,' said Littlefeet.

'Then it's certainly time that we did something about Bong,' said Gobo, frowning.

A small pixie called Dumbell began to giggle. The others stared at him. 'What's the matter?' asked Gobo.

'I've thought of something,' said

Dumbell. 'My aunt has a motor car, and when I'm good she lets me use it. Now what about me bringing it here, giving everyone but Bong a nice ride – and then leaving it somewhere for him to borrow.'

'What's the use of that?' said Gobo.

'We'll leave a runaway spell in the seat,' giggled Dumbell, 'and as soon as Bong gets in, the car will run away with him for miles and miles and miles! After a hundred miles it will tip him out, and come back here to us.'

The little folk stared at Dumbell in delight. It sounded a very good idea. Dumbell was at once sent off to borrow his aunt's car.

He soon came back in it, grinning all over his mischievous little face. He sounded the horn loudly and everyone came running out.

'I'll give you all rides in turn,' shouted Dumbell. So first Gobo got in and had a

ride, and then Littlefeet, and then Tiptoe. Mister Bong pushed his way through
the crowd after that, and shouted out that
he wanted a turn.

'Oh, no, I'm not giving *you* any rides!'
said Dumbell cheekily. 'I don't want my
car lost in the village pond, Mister Bong.
That's what you do with things that are
lent to you, isn't it?'

So Bong was not allowed a ride at all, and he was very angry indeed, for he felt sure he could drive the little red motor car just as well as Dumbell could.

'There!' said Dumbell, when everyone but Bong had had a nice drive round the village. 'That's all for today. I'll just put the car safely by this wall and go and have my supper.'

He put it beside a wall near Bong's house. Before he got out he pressed a runaway spell on to the driving-seat. It looked like a bit of yellow stamp-paper. Dumbell giggled, jumped out, and ran home to supper.

As soon as everyone was gone, Mister Bong ran out of his house. He went to the car, pleased to see it left so near his house. He got in and took hold of the wheel.

'I'll show Dumbell that I will have my
turn in the car just like everyone else!' he
said. He started off, and as soon as the

little folk heard the sound of the car, they
all rushed out of their houses to see what
would happen.

'Goodbye, Bong! Goodbye, Bong!'
they shouted, waving their hands in glee.

Bong looked surprised. He meant to go
once round the village, but somehow the
car wouldn't go the way he wanted it to.

The car ran to the main road. Bong
tried to turn it back to the village, but no,

it wouldn't turn. 'R-r-r-r-r-r-,' it went, as if it were laughing at him.

'Goodbye, and good riddance!' yelled the folk of Cherry Village. Bong began to feel frightened. He didn't seem to be driving the car at all – it seemed to be driving him! Off he went down the main road, up a hill, and down the other side, going faster and faster and faster.

The little folk could no longer see him.
They took hands and danced in a ring for
joy. 'He's gone, he's gone!' they sang.
'Now we shall all be happy again!'

That night, going rather slowly, as if it

were a little tired, the magic motor car
came back again to Cherry Village.
Everybody welcomed it. They patted its
bonnet, they tied a ribbon to its steering-
wheel, and really made a great fuss of it.

'Thank you!' they said. 'Thank you! We shan't see Mister Bong again!'

And they won't. He was tipped out on a rubbish-heap in Goblin town over a hundred miles away – and now he is a servant to a family of goblins. Well, it serves him right – he shouldn't have been such a nuisance!

ISBN 0-86163-731-3

Text copyright Darrell Waters Limited
Illustrations copyright © 1994 Award Publications Limited

Enid Blyton's signature is a trademark of Darrell Waters Limited

The Magic Motor Car first published in Enid Blyton's Lucky Story Book

This edition first published 1994 by Award Publications Limited,
Goodyear House, 52-56 Osnaburgh Street, London NW1 3NS

Printed in Italy